MOBY DICK

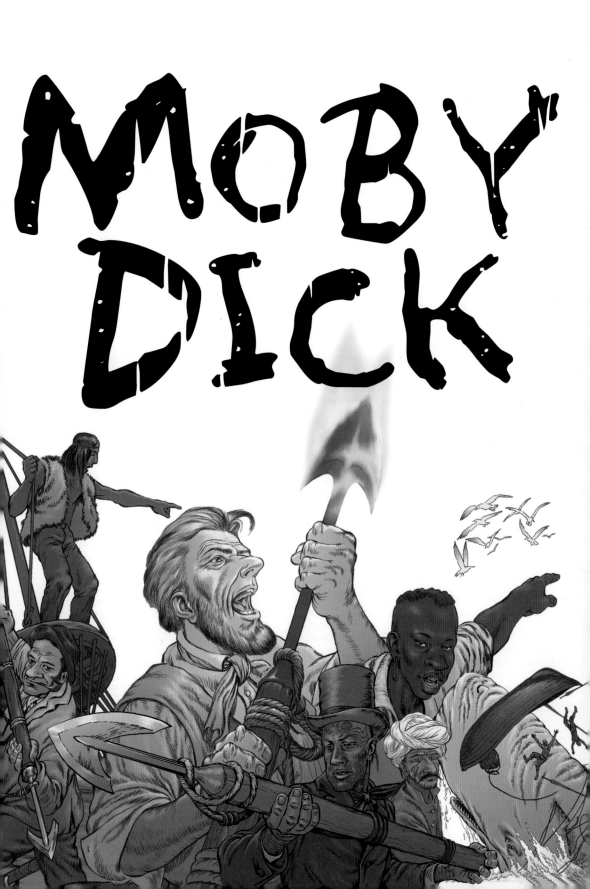

Acknowledgments:

Artists: Penko Gelev
Sotir Gelev

First edition for North America (including Canada and Mexico), Philippine Islands, and Puerto Rico published in 2007 by Barron's Educational Series, Inc.

All inquiries should be addressed to:
Barron's Educational Series, Inc.
250 Wireless Boulevard
Hauppauge, NY 11788
www.barronseduc.com

ISBN-13 (Hardcover): 978-0-7641-5977-0
ISBN-10 (Hardcover): 0-7641-5977-1
ISBN-13 (Paperback): 978-0-7641-3492-0
ISBN-10 (Paperback): 0-7641-3492-2

Library of Congress Control No.: 2005936254

Picture credits:
p40 The Art Archive/Culver Pictures
p41 Corbis
p44 TopFoto.co.uk
p45 The Art Archive/Global Book Publishing
p47 The Art Archive/Global Book Publishing
Every effort has been made to trace copyright holders. The Salariya Book Company apologizes
for any omissions and would be pleased, in such cases, to add an acknowledgment in future editions.

Printed and bound in China
9 8 7 6 5 4 3 2

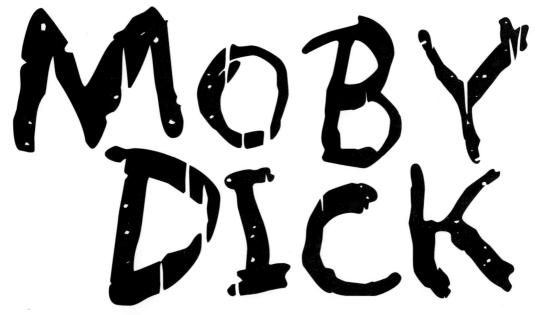

MOBY DICK

HERMAN MELVILLE

Illustrated by
Penko Gelev

BARRON'S

Retold by
Sophie Furse

Series created and designed by
David Salariya

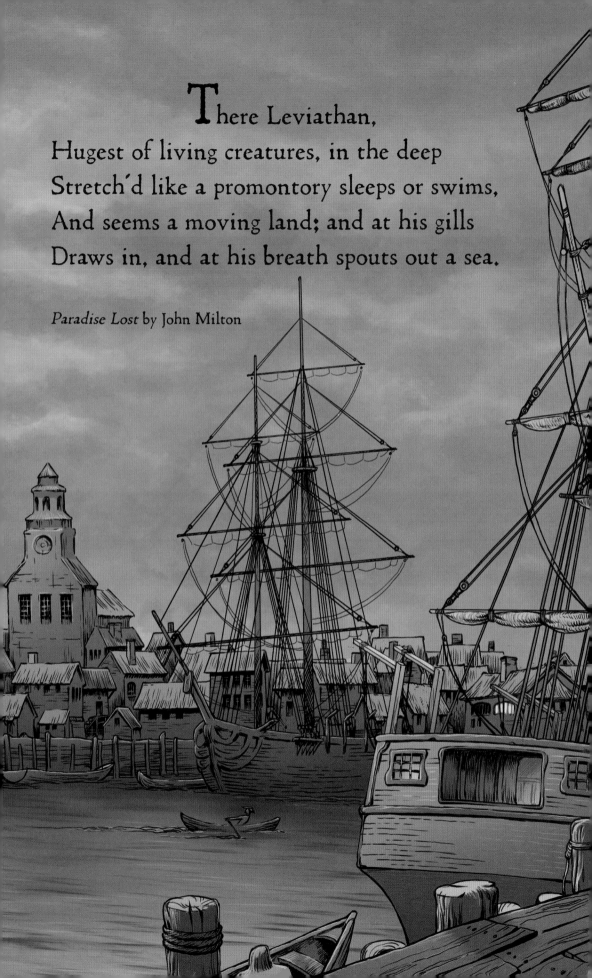

There Leviathan,
Hugest of living creatures, in the deep
Stretch'd like a promontory sleeps or swims,
And seems a moving land; and at his gills
Draws in, and at his breath spouts out a sea.

Paradise Lost by John Milton

CHARACTERS

Ishmael,
the narrator

Captain Ahab,
captain of the
Pequod

Queequeg,
harpooner

Stubb,
second mate

Fedallah

Starbuck,
first mate

Mrs. Hussey,
owner of
the Try Pots Inn

Tashtego,
harpooner

Captain Peleg,
co-owner of
the *Pequod*

Captain
Bildad,
co-owner of
the *Pequod*

Flask,
third mate

Daggoo,
harpooner

Elijah,
a mysterious stranger

Perth,
blacksmith

CALL ME ISHMAEL

It was a cold Saturday night when I arrived in New Bedford. I was on my way to Nantucket to join the crew of a whaling ship.

I heard a forlorn creaking and saw a sign outside the Spouter Inn.

The landlord told me I would have to share a bed with a harpooner. The night was bitter and I decided it was better to share half a decent man's blanket than to go elsewhere.

I was awakened by the arrival of the mysterious harpooner, carrying a candle in one hand and a bag in the other.

I was just summoning my courage to speak to him when he blew out the candle, lit his pipe, and leapt into bed! By now, sure he was a cannibal, I cried out in terror.

The landlord appeared and reassured me that Queequeg had no desire to eat me so, my mind at rest, I fell asleep.

In the morning, Queequeg leapt out of bed and told me he would dress first and leave me alone. He began to shave using not a razor, but his harpoon!

Breakfast was served and the other boarders all appeared to be whalemen, judging by their dress and tanned faces. Ignoring the bread and coffee the others were eating, my roommate reached over the table with his harpoon and speared a piece of bloody, almost raw meat.

CHRISTIANS AND CANNIBALS

It being a Sunday, I decided to visit the Whaleman's Chapel. I strolled through the town, noticing the houses of the wealthy, all paid for with profits from whaling.

Sleet was soon driving down. I followed the procession of sailors, sailor's wives, and sailor's widows into the chapel.

Yes, Ishmael, the same fate may be thine.[1]

I took my seat and looked around, surprised to see Queequeg. I began to read the marble memorials to the men lost at sea and felt saddened.

The doors opened and the legendary Father Mapple entered, shaking sleet from his coat.[2] (see notes below)

God had prepared a great fish to swallow up Jonah.

He took his place in the ship-like pulpit, and delivered a passionate sermon on the fitting subject of Jonah and the whale.[3]

Later on, I returned to the inn and found Queequeg there alone. Finding him considerably less terrifying by the light of day, I decided to get to know him better.

As we became better acquainted, Queequeg made me a gift of a shrunken head. A strange and ugly gift, but I felt pleased all the same by his generosity.

Next Queequeg solemnly divided his money into two equal piles and presented me with one, as a sign of our new friendship.

Later that night, in the same spirit of friendship, Queequeg invited me to take part in his pagan ceremony. Afterwards we talked and shared his pipe between us.

1. thine: Yours.
2. He had been a harpooner before becoming a priest.
3. In an Old Testament story, Jonah disobeyed God and was swallowed by a great fish before eventually being saved.

In his strange version of English he told me all about his home. I feel I now understand his story enough to retell it here.

Queequeg was originally from an island called Kokovoko. His father was the High Chief of a tribe of cannibals. One day, a whaling ship visited their island.

Having a spirit of adventure, Queequeg wanted to see the world and begged the captain to let him join the crew.

The ship was full, so he was refused. Did this rejection deter him? Not at all! He sailed his canoe out to meet the ship, then climbed up and onto the deck.

The captain was astonished and threatened to throw Queequeg overboard if he didn't return to his island.

But brave Queequeg grabbed hold of a ring and grasped it tightly, ignoring all the captain's threats.

The captain even threatened to cut Queequeg's hands off with a cutlass, but to no effect. Eventually the captain was forced to allow him to join the crew.

Queequeg and I now discussed our future plans and decided to join the same whaling ship. We would share any excitement and adventures that came our way.

NANTUCKET

It was late when we reached Nantucket, and, needing somewhere to spend the night, we found ourselves at the Try Pots Inn.[1] I thought that the two pots hanging outside looked eerily like a gallows awaiting doomed men.

The inn was owned by Hosea Hussey and his wife. They served a choice of fish chowders for breakfast, lunch, and dinner.[2] Hungry from our journey, we happily set about our meal.

Next morning I left Queequeg and Yojo, his idol, to a day of fasting while I went to find us a ship. Queequeg said Yojo foretold that I alone must select our vessel.

I soon heard of three vessels preparing for three-year voyages. Having looked at each in turn, I decided on the *Pequod*.

The ship itself was old-fashioned and rather small. Then I met one of the owners: old Captain Peleg.

> Want to see what whaling is, eh? Have ye clapped eye on Captain Ahab?

> What dost thou think of him, Bildad?

> He'll do.

> Blast ye, Captain Bildad!

I told him I wished to learn whaling and to see the world. He told me that Ahab was the present captain, whose leg had been eaten by a monstrous whale.

The other owner, Captain Bildad, then appeared. He and Peleg almost came to blows over what lay I should receive.[3]

---

1. try-pots: Pots in which whale blubber is boiled to extract the oil.
2. chowder: A thick, creamy soup often made with fish. It is often associated with New England.
3. lay: Share of the profits from a whaling vessel.

That evening . . .

Get the axe! For God's sake, run for the doctor, some one, while I pry it open!

Queequeg, what's the matter with you?

After knocking on Queequeg's door several times without answer, I began to worry. The door was locked from inside!

Mrs. Hussey and I were both quite sure Queequeg was dead. I burst through the door expecting the worst, but found him sitting calmly on the floor with Yojo on his head.

He's not been baptized right, or it would have washed some of that devil's blue off his face.[1]

You see him small drop of tar dere? Well, spose him one whale eye.

After breakfast, we made our way to the Pequod. Captain Peleg announced that he let no cannibal onboard unless they proved that they had converted to Christianity.

I did my best to reassure him. Satisfied, Peleg invited Queequeg onboard and asked if he'd ever struck a fish.

Immediately, Queequeg jumped up and aimed his harpoon at a point on the dock.

We must have Hedgehog there, I mean Quohog, in one of our boats.

He darted the harpoon and struck the very same spot of glistening tar he'd pointed to! Peleg and Bildad were awestruck, and almost fell over each other to get the ship's papers for Queequeg to sign.

Realizing the benefits of such an exact harpooner, Peleg asked him to sign, but seemed to stumble over Queequeg's name.

Queequeg took the offered quill, and made a strange figure on the paper; a symbol I later learned meant "infinity."[2]

1. devil's blue: Queequeg's tattoos.
2. quill: A bird's feather made into a pen for writing.

SETTING SAIL

We had just left the ship and were strolling along peacefully when a stranger stopped to ask if we had shipped in the Pequod.[1] He was shabbily dressed and had only one arm. He seemed very strange.

Deciding he must be mad, we tried to leave. But the stranger called us back and asked if we had met Captain Ahab. The man said his name was Elijah, which I hoped was not an ill omen.[2]

For several days there was great activity aboard as the *Pequod* was prepared. The sails were mended and supplies for the long voyage were brought on board.

Dawn the next day was gray and misty as Queequeg and I went to the docks. We saw the mysterious Elijah again, and once more his strange words unsettled me, because they seemed to make no sense.

We finally boarded the Pequod where everything seemed to be quiet. My encounter with Elijah must have affected me, as once or twice I thought I saw shadows moving just out of sight. I tried to shake off a feeling of uneasiness.

1. shipped: Joined the crew.
2. Elijah: The name of an Old Testament prophet who foretold the death of the evil King Ahab.

Suddenly we came across a man face down and sound asleep. As he seemed to be the only other soul aboard, I suggested we sit and wait. So without further ado, Queequeg prodded the man and sat down upon his back!

Queequeg told me that as there were no sofas in his native land, his father the king would often fatten his servants to make them more comfortable to sit on.

I told Queequeg to get off, which he did. Then he lit his pipe and we shared it. The sleeper awoke and I told him that we were part of the crew.

Later, among all the hustle and bustle, I saw old Captain Bildad pacing the deck, reluctant to go.

Eventually Captains Bildad and Peleg clambered into their small boat to return to shore and our voyage finally got underway.

A cold, damp breeze was blowing and, with a chorus of cheering, we set sail into the lonely Atlantic.

It seemed odd that Captain Ahab should stay unseen in his cabin – but he did. We saw no sign of him for several days.

Captain Ahab

Captain Ahab was tall and broad-shouldered, and in place of the leg he'd lost was an ivory peg, carved from the jaw of a sperm whale.

Ahab slotted his leg into holes in the deck to stop himself from slipping.

If ye see a white one, split your lungs for him![1]

Next morning, second mate Stubb advised Flask, the third mate, not to speak harshly to Ahab, no matter what. He then warned him to look out for a white whale.

For lunch, we gathered around the crew's table and Dough-Boy the steward served us. Daggoo (another harpooner) was forced to sit on the floor because he was too tall to sit at the table!

Come here, so we may pick your bones clean!

Dough-Boy was nervous serving the cannibals, Queequeg and Tashtego. They teased and jabbed at him mercilessly.

Skin your eyes for him, men; look sharp for white water.[2]

One morning after breakfast, Ahab nailed a gold doubloon to the mast.[3] It was for the first man to catch a white whale with a wrinkled brow and a crooked jaw.

That white whale must be the same that some call Moby Dick.

Ahab confirmed that the white whale was indeed Moby Dick. The First Mate, Starbuck, then asked if it was Moby Dick who had taken Ahab's leg. Ahab confirmed it, swearing to get his revenge.

Starbuck called Ahab's obsession with the whale madness. But Ahab, filled with a passion, ordered the harpooners to remove the barbed iron ends from their poles and fill them with liquor.

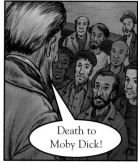

Death to Moby Dick!

He ordered the harpooners to drink, and swear an oath to kill Moby Dick. Turning to the rest of the crew, he called upon us to do the same.

1. split your lungs: Shout as loudly as possible.
2. white water: A sign that a whale is present.
3. gold doubloon: a gold coin.

Captain Ahab retired to his cabin. He knew the crew thought he was mad, but he swore to kill the whale no matter what.

I had shouted my oath along with the rest of the crew, and yet I knew nothing of the whale. Wild rumors circulated among the men, who told me how Ahab had come to lose his leg.

Surrounded by the wrecks of three boats, and with his men and oars stranded, Ahab had battled the whale.

He seized a large knife and bravely lunged forward, trying to stab Moby Dick to death.

But as the whale's sickle-shaped jaw swept by, it severed Ahab's leg like a mower cutting grass.

In his pain and fury, Ahab had raved about the white whale, blaming him for all the evils in the world. Gripped by madness, the captain was secured in a strait-jacket by the crew. [2]

After some time, Ahab took over the ship again and began to issue orders once more. But the madness still lurked beneath the surface.

In his cabin onboard the *Pequod*, Ahab studied his large sea charts. He had chosen to set sail earlier in the year than normal so that he could spend extra time hunting Moby Dick.

---

1. dismember: Remove part of the whale that took his leg.
2. strait-jacket: A jacket with very long sleeves used to restrain violent movement.

"THERE SHE BLOWS!"

It was a warm, lazy afternoon. Queequeg and I were weaving a sword-mat when I heard Tashtego shout out in excitement.[1] It was our first sighting of whales!

Immediately, the crew sprang into action. Tashtego scrambled down from watch and Ahab quickly ordered the crew to the boats.

Suddenly, five strangers appeared seemingly from thin air! These men were Ahab's personal boat crew, their existence kept secret from the rest of us, who stared in amazement at the strangers.

Ahab ignored our surprise and ordered the boats lowered.

One of these strangers, Fedallah, seemed to be their leader. He oversaw the others casting loose the tackles and set off.

Three more boats took to the water and followed Ahab's craft. I took my place in the final boat, led by Starbuck, with Queequeg as our harpooner.

Without warning, a mist descended and the sea became rough, making it difficult to see.

In another boat, Flask climbed onto the giant Daggoo's shoulders to try to see into the distance.

1. sword-mat: A tightly woven mat.

The wind was fierce and we were swept along at maddening speeds. The whales seemed all around and our boats split up to chase them.

At last, a whale surfaced near us. Fearless Queequeg seized his chance and threw his harpoon.

There she breaches! The white whale, the white whale!

Waves swamped the boat and we were tossed out into the squall.[1] But the whale, only grazed by Queequeg's iron, escaped, and we clambered back into the boat, wet and cold.

One morning, Daggoo saw a white shape in the distance. He saw it rise and fall several times, and excitedly called out that he saw Moby Dick. Soon the small boats were in pursuit.

However as we drew nearer, I saw that it was not Moby Dick but a giant squid, its long tentacles trailing in the water. The squid seemed like a ghost, and with a sucking sound, sank beneath the waves.

The great live squid, which they say few whaleships have beheld and returned to their ports to tell of it.

The squid had a strange effect on Starbuck, who gazed at the spot where it had disappeared for some time. He said he almost wished he'd seen Moby Dick instead.

STUBB'S SUPPER

Queequeg also thought the great squid was a sign, but he thought it meant sperm whales were nearby.

On my watch, I saw a gigantic sperm whale break the surface, the sun shining on his broad back. I instantly called out.

Ahab ordered the boats out and the crew erupted in excited shouts. The noise alarmed the whale and it turned to swim away. Ahab ordered us to speak only in whispers, and so we paddled after our prey in silence.

As the whale surfaced Stubb struck at it, turning the sea red. Finally, it blew out a spout of blood-tinged water and died.

The whale had been killed some distance from the *Pequod,* so three of the boats began to drag it back. My arms were fit to drop off by the time we arrived with our cargo.

To my surprise, Ahab seemed indifferent to our catch, as if it reminded him that Moby Dick still lived.[2] He gave orders to secure the carcass to the side of the ship and then retired for the night.

Stubb loved whale steaks, and sent Daggoo to cut him one. By the time Stubb sat down to his strange supper it was almost midnight.

The terrible noise of hungry sharks tearing at the whale carcass, and the slap of their tails against the hull, was surely enough to terrify the sleepers down below deck.

1. Both pipes smoked out: Stubb's pipe burned out at the same time that the whale died.
2. indifferent: Uninterested.

Stop dat smacking ob de lips!

Stubb liked to joke and asked the cook, Fleece, to tell the sharks to be quiet because he could hardly think.

We took turns to drive the sharks away – or they would soon eat the whole whale. We killed some, and the sea was soon a frenzy of sharks feeding on each other.

Aaaarggh!

Queequeg pulled a shark onto deck to skin it, but the shark was not dead and almost bit poor Queequeg's hand off!

We set to work removing the blubber from the whale's carcass. Once a strip of blubber is freed, the whale is peeled in sections, much like peeling an orange. The huge white remains of the whale were then cut adrift, and were set upon almost immediately by sharks and dozens of screaming seabirds.

ANGELS AND DEVILS

After several days, another whaling ship was spotted in the distance – the *Jeroboam* from Nantucket. It lowered a boat, which soon drew alongside the *Pequod*.

The *Jeroboam*'s Captain Mayhew said there was a contagious epidemic onboard and he was fearful of infecting us.[1]

That's he! that's he!

Stubb recognized the other man as one who had claimed to be a great prophet before joining the *Jeroboam*.

This man had said that he was the archangel Gabriel, and promptly ordered the captain to jump overboard. He was now so powerful the captain had to keep him aboard.

Ahab told Mayhew that he did not fear their epidemic and invited him aboard, but Gabriel objected. All Ahab was interested in was news of Moby Dick, though, and he began to question the two sailors.

Hast thou seen the white whale?

The conversation was difficult as the waves kept pushing the small boat away. Mayhew and Gabriel had to keep rowing back.

Macey disappeared!

Mayhew told a bleak tale about Moby Dick. A former crewman named Macey was killed when the whale tossed him from his boat, never to be seen again.

1. epidemic: An infectious disease that is widespread in a particular area.

Gabriel claimed this death was an omen. He had warned against pursuing Moby Dick, but Macey wouldn't listen, and so had died.

Ahab remembered a letter onboard for the *Jeroboam* and tried to pass it over. It was for Macey.

But Gabriel grabbed the letter, and, piercing it with a knife, threw both to land at Ahab's feet. Then the *Jeroboam*'s small boat sped away.

This episode over, life returned to normal. After several days, Ahab spotted a right whale and sent Stubb and Flask to catch it. Right whales were thought inferior catches, so the men were confused at Ahab's orders.[1]

Flask explained that he'd heard Fedallah say that a ship with a sperm whale's head on one side and a right whale's head on the other would never capsize.

He wondered why Ahab had anything to do with Fedallah. Stubb then said he believed Ahab had sold his soul to him to catch Moby Dick.

1. right whales: Slow-moving whales that were hunted for their blubber.

A Lucky Escape

The sperm whale's head lashed to one side caused the *Pequod* to list severely. By adding the right whale's head, we soon regained our balance.

Tashtego climbed onto the sperm whale to "tap the tun."[1] He carefully cut a hole and began collecting the valuable whale oil in a bucket.

Suddenly, Tashtego slipped and disappeared head-first into the hole!

Aaagh!

Man overboard!

Daggoo tried to pass a bucket down so Tashtego could climb out. But his extra weight sent the whale's head crashing into the sea, where it immediately began to sink.

We heard another loud splash as brave Queequeg, sword in hand, dived in to rescue Tashtego. We rushed to the side of the ship, eager for signs of life.

Soon Daggoo shouted that he saw them. Queequeg had dived under the whale's head, cut a hole in the bottom and then dragged Tashtego out by his long hair.

Later we encountered a German whaling vessel called the *Jungfrau*. They seemed eager to speak with us and sent across their captain, Derick De Beer.

1. tun: Removing the oil from the whale's head. A tun is also the name of a barrel or cask for wine or beer.

De Beer came begging for lamp oil and Ahab was so eager for news of Moby Dick that he let him aboard. But De Beer knew nothing.

As De Beer headed back to the *Jungfrau,* a pod of whales was spotted.[1] We saw an old bull whale swimming much slower than the others, and, as we drew closer, we saw that this ancient creature only had one fin.

Better luck next time!

Sure of his crew's triumph, De Beer taunted us, much to Starbuck's fury. But unluckily for him, he nearly capsized, and we took the lead.

Our harpooners leapt up and their barbs all struck the old whale. Our boats were pulled forward and we sailed right ahead of the Germans.

So it was that the *Pequod* claimed the carcass of that crippled old whale.

Who darted that stone lance? And when? Was it before America was even discovered?

Under the whale's skin we found a corroded harpoon from a previous hunt. We also discovered a stone harpoon-head, with the wound long healed. That made me wonder at the age of this creature.

But our efforts to secure the whale ended in failure – the carcass seemed determined to sink. Finally, we were forced to cut the lines and release the body of the ancient whale, in case he dragged us down.

1. pod: The name for a group of whales.

THE ROSE-BUD

In time we reached waters popular with sperm whales, and Ahab's hope of finding Moby Dick grew. So desperate was he that he opted not to stop to take on more fresh water.

We saw a continuous chain of whale-jets sparkling in the air. The crew crowded into the boats and we gave chase, driving the whales ahead of us.

When whales are plentiful, the aim is to kill as many as possible, or at least to injure them so that you may kill them at a later time.

To do this, we used druggs.[1] This extra weight made it much more difficult for harpooned whales to escape.

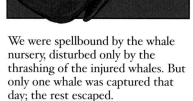

They are amazing creatures.

The cows and calves seemed fearless, and came right up to the boats like dogs. It was wonderful to watch these mighty creatures so closely and in such peace.

We were spellbound by the whale nursery, disturbed only by the thrashing of the injured whales. But only one whale was captured that day; the rest escaped.

Another loss that day was Queequeg's hat, which was knocked from his head and never seen again.

1. druggs: Blocks of wood that could be fastened to harpoons.

We came across a French ship, the *Rose-Bud,* with two whales strapped to the sides. The stench was disgusting, and Stubb wondered if one of the whales contained ambergris.[1]

Stubb decided to try to trick the French crew into abandoning their whales. Holding his nose, he called out to a French crewman. This man was not happy with the stench, so Stubb used him to trick their captain.

The crew kept climbing up the masts for fresher air. Using the crewman to translate, Stubb told the captain that the whales carried a fever which would kill the crew. Terrified, the inexperienced captain ordered the carcasses cut free.

Generous Stubb offered to help by towing one carcass away himself. He was pleased to have secured the possible source of valuable ambergris for the *Pequod*.

Thrusting his hands into the whale, he pulled out something that appeared to be ripe old cheese, but it was worth a fortune!

As Ahab often paced the quarter-deck he gazed at his doubloon. He announced his intention that the white whale be raised from the sea within a month and a day.

---

1. ambergris: A foul-smelling, waxy substance produced by some sperm whales. It was very valuable and used in perfume manufacture.
2. If the French crewman helps Stubb, he won't have to continue working with the stinking dead whales.

News of the White Whale

Now in popular whaling waters, we saw an English whaler, the *Samuel Enderby*. Ahab hailed them, hoping for news of Moby Dick.

Captain Boomer said that indeed they saw the white whale last season, and that it cost him his arm.

While trying to catch a harpooned whale, a huge whale with a wrinkled white head had appeared. It tried to bite through the harpoon line, but became tangled in it.

Boomer's boat had then attacked Moby Dick, but he thrashed about, bringing the line down across the boat and slicing it in two.[1] The crew was pitched into the sea.

Boomer tried to grab hold of the iron – harpoons from Ahab's previous attack – stuck in the whale's side.

Then, tragedy! Another harpoon flew forward and pierced Boomer's arm. He was pinned to the whale and thought he would drown. But then it came free.

At this point the ship's doctor took over the story. For days Boomer's wound grew worse, until the doctor was forced to remove his arm. But Ahab didn't care, he just wanted to know more about Moby Dick.

Boomer confessed they had seen the whale twice since then, but feeling that the loss of one arm was enough, didn't give chase. Dr. Bunger warned Ahab that Moby Dick was best left alone, but realized that Ahab was obsessed with it.

Ahab didn't care for the warning either, and, learning that the white whale had headed east, called his crew back to the boat, and we returned to the *Pequod*.

1. line: The rope attached to the harpoons.

Let it leak! I'm all aleak myself. Aye! Leaks in leaks!

The next morning . . .

There is one God that is Lord over the earth, and one Captain that is lord over the *Pequod*.

Starbuck reported that the casks were leaking, and we could lose more whale oil in an hour than we could catch in a year.

Starbuck argued, but Ahab ordered him to leave his cabin, pointing a loaded musket at him. Starbuck told Ahab that his greatest threat came from Ahab himself.

In the midst of this, my friend Queequeg had come down with a fever, and each day seemed closer to death. He wasted away, becoming thinner and thinner.

Queequeg said he'd like to be buried in a canoe, as was his island's custom. The carpenter was called for to make Queequeg's coffin – the closest we could get to a canoe.

Queequeg climbed into his coffin with his harpoon and little wooden idol, but slowly he seemed to rally and returned to health.

He later said that if a man made up his mind to live, mere sickness couldn't kill him. The coffin was not wasted, though, because Queequeg used it as a sea chest.

For the white fiend!

Ego non baptizo te in nomine patris, sed in nomine diaboli![2]

Ahab asked Perth, the blacksmith, if he could make a special harpoon to kill Moby Dick. Perth made many different blades until finally the old man was satisfied.

Ahab said the harpoon must be tempered with the blood of the harpooners, Queequeg, Tashtego, and Daggoo.[1] They each cut their arms, letting the blood flow onto the barb.

Ahab seemed crazed at this point, and as the blood touched the iron, he howled out what was both a prayer and a curse over this strange baptism.

1. tempered: Improve the hardness or flexibility of metal by heating it and adding substances to it.
2. This is Latin for: I baptise you not in the name of the father, but in the name of the devil!

THE PROPHECY

Have I not said, old man, that neither hearse nor coffin can be thine?

I have dreamed it again.

We then caught and killed four whales, but one was so far from the *Pequod* that Ahab's small boat had to stay with it to prevent it being stolen or eaten.

Fedallah watched the sharks circling the carcass. Ahab awoke, and reported dreams about hearses and coffins.

Then Fedallah made an incredible prophecy to Captain Ahab.[1]

. . . wood of the last one must be grown in America.

I shall still go before thee, thy pilot.

I am immortal then, on land and on sea.

Fedallah said that Ahab must see two hearses before he could die – the first not made by mortal hands, and the second made of wood from America.

Fedallah also said he would die first, but reappear later as a guide. At first, Ahab was amused.

Finally Fedallah told Ahab that only hemp could kill him, which Ahab took to mean the gallows.[2] Sure that nothing could kill him, he laughed.

Oh! Jolly is the gale, And a joker is the whale, A'flourishin' his tail...

Sailing in tropical waters meant fearsome storms were common and, sure enough, one night the *Pequod* was caught in a typhoon. The main sails tore and the ship was tossed about in the huge waves, but Stubb calmly sang a song.

1. prophecy: Predicting events that are yet to occur.
2: hemp: Plant fibers used to make rope.

Look aloft! The corpusants![1]

Lightning flashed, thunder crashed, and Ahab felt the storm was leading him to the white whale. Suddenly, Starbuck called out for us to look up at the yardarms. To my amazement, the three main masts were all tipped with ghostly flames!

The scar on Ahab's face had been caused by lightning and he seemed to pray to the spirit of the flames. Suddenly his harpoon was hit by lightning and flames erupted.

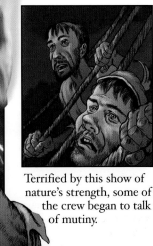

Terrified by this show of nature's strength, some of the crew began to talk of mutiny.

All your oaths to hunt the white whale are as binding as mine.

Hearing this, Ahab raised his still burning harpoon, and, waving it among his mutinous and wretched crew, he threatened to impale the first man to leave his post.

The crew fell back, and fiery Ahab reminded them of the oath they had all sworn to kill Moby Dick. This said, Ahab put out the flame and plunged us into darkness.

1. corpusants: Balls of light sometimes seen near the masts of ships during a storm, possibly ball lightning.

AFTER THE STORM

After midnight, the typhoon finally grew calm. In such a storm it was common for the compass needles to spin, making it impossible to steer accurately.

Shall this crazed old man be suffered to drag a whole ship's company to doom with him?

Starbuck entered Ahab's room to tell him this, and saw a pair of loaded muskets in a rack upon the wall.

A touch, and Starbuck may survive to hug his wife and child again.

Taking a musket in his shaking hand, Starbuck walked toward Ahab's hammock. He remembered Ahab's oath and his threats to the crew.

Oh, Moby Dick, I clutch thy heart at last.

Ahab stirred restlessly, dreaming of the whale, and Starbuck realized he could not murder him.

After steadying his hand, Starbuck replaced the musket and returned to the deck with a heavy heart.

Thou liest!

East-sou-east, sir.

The next morning, as Ahab silently watched the rising sun, he suddenly hurried toward the helm and asked in which direction the ship was heading.

We were heading in the wrong direction! By the position of the sun, Ahab realized that the compass needles had been inverted by the storm.[1]

Out of this bit of steel Ahab can make one of his own that will point as true as any.

He immediately changed course and asked for a sailmaker's needle and an old lance. It was thought bad luck by sailors to sail using inverted needles, so Ahab made a new compass.

The sun is East, and that compass swears it!

30   1. inverted: Opposite to the normal position.

Those are the voices of newly drowned men in the sea.

Near the Equator, we passed a cluster of rocky islets from which came an unearthly sound. Some said it was mermaids, but the Manxman, the oldest sailor onboard, said they were ghostly voices.[1]

These islets were also popular with seals – another bad omen. This added to the uneasiness on the voyage.

Aaaarrgggh!

The tension grew again when early one morning, an unfortunate sailor climbed the mast, lost his hold, and fell into the sea.

A life-buoy was quickly thrown in after him. I wondered if perhaps the sailor was still half-asleep when he had climbed the mast.

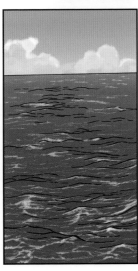

But it was no use. The life-buoy, dried out by the hot sun, filled with water and soon followed the sailor to the bottom of the sea.

This crew was nervous and now quite sure that evil signs were warning them against the pursuit of the white whale. The lost life-buoy needed to be replaced, so Queequeg offered his coffin to be made into a new one.

1. Manxman: Someone from the Isle of Man.

Lost at Sea

Next morning a fast-moving ship, the *Rachel*, drew alongside and hailed us. Ahab immediately asked if they had seen Moby Dick, and Captain Gardiner said yes.

He asked us to help find his missing whale-boat. Stubb was skeptical about why we should help, and voiced his suspicions.[1]

The day before, Gardiner's ship had seen Moby Dick. Most of the boats were already miles away, so the last was lowered with his son onboard, and had not been seen since.

Gardiner begged to charter the *Pequod* for two days to search for his son's boat.[2] He appealed to Ahab to take pity and help him, but Ahab hard-heartedly refused.

Shocked by Ahab's refusal, the crew's good humor vanished. Convinced that he wouldn't be told if Moby Dick was sighted, Ahab had Starbuck hoist him up the main mast.

From this viewpoint, Ahab could see for miles around. He gazed so intently at the horizon for a sign of Moby's spout, that he failed to see a seahawk approaching him.

The hawk came closer, and grabbed Ahab's hat in its sharp, curved talons, and flew off.

Ahab's hat was gone! We saw a black spot falling from a great height as the bird finally dropped it.

1. skeptical: Suspicious and disbelieving.
2. charter: Hiring a boat.

32

The mood onboard did not improve as we sailed on. Soon, we came upon a ship miserably misnamed the *Delight*. On its side was the shattered remains of a whale-boat.

Hast seen the white whale? Hast killed him?

Assuming that the damage was caused by Moby Dick, Ahab feverishly asked the captain for news.

The harpoon is not yet forged that ever will do that.

The captain confirmed both that Moby Dick was responsible . . . and that he still lived.

Tempered in blood, and tempered by lightning are these barbs.

Hearing this, Ahab grabbed Perth's harpoon, and showed it to the *Delight*'s captain. He promised that this was the one to kill Moby Dick.

Are ye ready there?

The captain wished Ahab luck and returned to the funeral of one of the men killed by Moby Dick – the only body they had managed to recover.

As we left, we heard a splash as the dead man, sewn inside his hammock, hit the sea.

Forty years of continual whaling! Forty years on the pitiless sea!

Starbuck sensed a deep sadness in his captain, as Ahab remembered the day he struck his first whale when he was just 18 years old. He confessed that of the past 40 years, he had spent most of it at sea.

My captain! Let us fly these deadly waters! Let us home!

Ahab admitted that his wife became a widow soon after they were wed. When he questioned his pursuit of Moby Dick, Starbuck begged him to turn back.

Is Ahab, Ahab? Is it I, God, or who, that lifts this arm?

But Starbuck's hopes were dashed once and for all, as Ahab spoke passionately about being commanded beyond his power to chase the white whale to the ends of the earth.

THE CHASE

That same night, Ahab ordered the crew to prepare for the chase. He felt certain that Moby Dick was near, and was desperate to be ready.

Ahab was being hoisted up the mast when he let out a terrific cry. In an instant, the other lookouts shouted . . . it was Moby Dick!

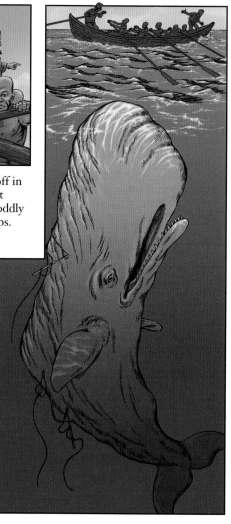

Ahab thought it was a good omen that he spotted the whale, and therefore kept the doubloon himself.

Led by Ahab, three boats set off in the direction of the whale's last spout. Fedallah's eyes seemed oddly bright, and he chewed at his lips.

A flock of birds around Ahab's boat alerted him to the whale below them. As he peered down into the water he saw a tiny white spot in the deep that grew larger by the second.

He tried desperately to steer out of the way as Moby Dick broke the surface, mouth gaping. The boat was bitten in half! Ahab was tipped into the sea, while the whale lashed the waves higher with his tail.

Moby Dick seemed to be swimming in circles, trying to create a whirlpool. Ahab narrowly escaped, and swam to Stubb's boat where he lay panting.

Ahab rubbed his bloodshot eyes and his first question was not about his crew, but his harpoon.

Assured that both his harpoon and his crew were safe, Ahab made haste back toward the safety of the *Pequod*.

Back onboard, Ahab assumed a state of readiness; alert and scanning the waves for a sign of Moby Dick. Seeing nothing, he went to examine the wreck of the whale-boat.

Starbuck warned him that losing any whale-boat was unlucky, but as it was the captain's own boat it was a particularly bad omen.

Ahab, however, dismissed these concerns as nonsense. He ordered Starbuck to resume the search for Moby Dick, but to be careful not to attack during the night.

35

MOBY DICK

At dawn . . .

The next morning, we spotted Moby Dick, still trailing the harpoons of other long-gone crews, as well as Ahab's. The boats were lowered and the chase began.

The boats were moving fast, but instead of fleeing, Moby Dick turned and swam toward them. Ahab cheered his men on, saying he would take the whale head-on, but almost immediately the whale charged!

The huge white whale seemed not to notice the many harpoons that stabbed and tore into his flesh.

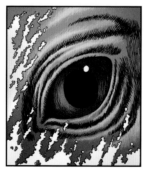

Aaargh!

He seemed to focus on the total destruction of each of the whale-boats and the men within them.

Although wounded, the diabolic creature cunningly used the lines to tangle and smash the boats against one another.[1]

Ahab's boat was flipped over the whale's head, tipping men into the sea. Victoriously, Moby Dick swam lazily away, trailing lines behind him. Ahab swam back to the *Pequod*.

All eyes fell on Ahab whose ivory leg had snapped off.

It was soon noticed that Fedallah was missing. Stubb said that he had become tangled in Ahab's line and was dragged down below the waves.

Ahab remembered Fedallah's prophecy that he would die first. It then seemed to Ahab that it was his destiny to continue on his quest.

The mood on the *Pequod* was solemn. The next day would be crucial, so work continued sharpening the harpoons. The sound of hammering lasted through the night.

In the meantime, Perth the carpenter set to work making another leg for Ahab. In the distance, Moby Dick remained in sight until the sun set.

A Prophecy Fulfilled

Dawn broke on another fair day, although the crew was still tense with anticipation. At last Ahab saw the spout, and instantly the three lookouts called out, too.

As the whale-boats descended, Ahab looked around and called Starbuck to him. Ahab offered his hand, and Starbuck, touched by the old man's nobility, begged him again not to go. But Ahab could not be persuaded.

As the boats pulled away, Starbuck called out – Ahab's boat was ringed by sharks! Ignoring the other boats, the sharks surrounded Ahab's, but the old man did not hear the warning.

Moby Dick rose up from the sea and we saw the irons from yesterday's attack dotted over his huge body.[1] A shout went up and there, caught in the lines that trailed from the whale, was the body of Fedallah.

Astonished, the harpoon fell from Ahab's hand as he remembered the prophecy: "I will reappear to guide you." Then he ordered us to get ready to attack.

Ahab's boat came alongside the whale and he stabbed his harpoon deep into Moby Dick's side. Thrashing around in pain, the whale managed to sink Ahab's boat for a third time before heading for the *Pequod*.

1. irons: Harpoons.

Ahab joined another boat and urged us to quickly return to the ship. But it was too late.

The whale smashed into the side of the *Pequod* and water flooded in. As it began to sink, Ahab realized his own ship was the second hearse of Fedallah's prophecy. He made a final, desperate stab at Moby Dick.

Bending over to clear the harpoon's line, a flying rope caught Ahab around the neck and, in an instant, he was gone.

For a moment we stood in shocked silence, watching the *Pequod* sinking fast. The hull was already beneath the waves.

Suddenly the pull of the sinking ship began to drag at the boats and they started to spin. This vortex soon pulled the boats, oars, and all the men downward and out of sight.[1] Fate chose to save me alone.

I watched this scene of horror while clinging onto Queequeg's coffin. I stayed like this for a day and a night until the *Rachel*, still searching for her missing children, found another orphan.

THE END

---

1. vortex: A whirling or spiralling movement of water.

HERMAN MELVILLE (1819 – 1891)

Herman Melville was born on August 1, 1819, in New York. His father, Allan Melville, was an import merchant trading in such items as handkerchiefs, scarves, and ribbons. His business was not thriving, but Allan was a dreamer who continually believed success was just around the corner and frequently moved his family into larger and larger houses to make it appear that business was booming. Finally, in October 1830, with his business in ruins, the Melville family (with eight children) travelled to Albany, New York, where Allan was forced to beg his brother-in-law for financial help.

Herman Melville....Photographed in 1885

EDUCATION

In 1832, Allan caught pneumonia. His delirium in the final days before his death is thought to have inspired the image of Captain Ahab raving in his hammock. After this, Herman and his elder brother, Gansevoort, stopped attending school and were sent out to work to support their family. It wasn't thought a terrible loss for Herman's schooling to end – he was a terrible speller and was not considered an outstanding student. From this point on, he was self-educated. After a failed attempt to become a surveyor and a brief spell as a teacher, Melville returned to New York feeling restless and in search of adventure.

SEA TRAVELS

On June 15, 1839, Melville set sail for Liverpool, England, on the *St. Lawrence*. The crew list contains an entry for a "Norman Melville" – possibly a result of his poor handwriting. It was then that he decided to join the crew of a whaling ship. He set out for New Bedford and on January 3, 1841, set sail on the *Acushnet*, a whaler bound for the Pacific Ocean. In July 1841, the *Acushnet* arrived at Nukuheva in the South Pacific. Melville promptly deserted and spent a month there in the Typee Valley. Typee warriors were ferocious; there were rumors of cannibalism. Their bodies were covered with tattoos marking battle victories, and it is possible this experience inspired the character of the tattooed harpooner Queequeg. Melville then joined the crew of an Australian whaler, arrived in Tahiti in

September 1842, and was promptly imprisoned as a mutineer. Released after a few weeks, Melville continued his travels before finally returning to America in 1844.

MELVILLE, THE WRITER

Upon his return home, Melville delighted his friends and family with tales of his adventures and set about writing them down for a wider audience. His first novel, *Typee*, was rejected by American publishers because it was thought too fantastic to be true, so Gansevoort took it to London in search of a publisher. He succeeded, and *Typee* was published in England in March 1846 and America in August of the same year.

MOBY-DICK

Melville had first heard an account of a real whaling ship tragedy while aboard the *Acushnet*. The *Essex* had been rammed and sunk by a large sperm whale in 1820 and Melville drew upon Owen Chase's account of his survival while writing *Moby-Dick*. He had also heard reports of an old albino whale named Mocha Dick, (named after the island of Mocha near Chile). This white whale was said to repeatedly turn and attack its hunters. *Moby-Dick* was published in 1851. In Britain it was split into three volumes entitled *The Whale*; in America it was published as a single novel called *Moby-Dick* or *The Whale*.[1]

AFTER *MOBY-DICK*

In spite of his reputation today as one of America's finest writers, Herman Melville only wrote from 1845 to 1857. Sadly, he never achieved the critical or financial success as a writer he hoped for, and in later life turned to writing poetry, much of which were unpublished during his lifetime. After 1857, money problems caused Melville to seek a living on the lecture circuit. However, he had a very quiet speaking voice, and after three years he gave it up. Melville's later years were marked by great personal tragedy. Both his sons died before him: Malcolm shot himself in 1867 and Stanwix died in 1886. His final novel, *Billy Budd*, was unfinished when he died in 1891, and remained unpublished until 1924.

Herman Melville and his wife are buried next to each other in Woodlawn Cemetery, New York.

---

1. The original title of the novel is hyphenated, although the whale's name throughout is not.

Timeline of Events

During the Lifetime of Herman Melville

1819
August 1st – Herman Melvill born in New York, second son of Allan and Maria Melvill (Maria added the final "e" to the surname later).

1825-29
Melville attends New York Male High School.

1830
Allan Melville's import business fails and the family moves to Albany, New York.

1831
English naturalist Charles Darwin sets sail on *HMS Beagle*.

1832
Allan Melville dies bankrupt. Maria is left to raise eight children single handed. Maria adds an "e" to their surname. Herman and his older brother are pulled out of school to help support the family.

1832-1834
Melville works as a clerk for New York State Bank in Albany.

1838
Melville and his family move to Lansingburgh, NY, where he studies surveying at Lansingburgh Academy.

1839
May – *Sketches from a Writing Desk* is published in two local newspapers, the "Democratic Press" and the "Lansingburgh Advertiser."
June 5th – Melville leaves New York on the *St. Lawrence*, bound for Liverpool, England.

1841
January 3rd – Melville joins the crew of the whaling ship *Acushnet* as a cabin boy on its maiden voyage for the South Seas.

1842
July 9th – Melville deserts *Acushnet* in the Marquesa Islands.
August 9th – Joins the Australian whaling ship *Lucy Ann*. He is accused of mutiny and imprisoned at Tahiti with others.
November 7th – Sails on the Nantucket whaling ship, *Charles and Henry*.

1843
August 9th   Joins the U.S. Navy and sails on the frigate *United States*.
October 14th – Discharged from the Navy and returns to Lansingburgh.

1846
Typee, an account of Melville's travels, is published and is the most popular of Melville's works during his lifetime.

1847
Omoo, the sequel to *Typee*, is published.
August 4th – Melville marries Elizabeth Shaw, daughter of the chief justice of Massachusetts' Supreme Court, and they move to Manhattan.

1849
Mardi and A Voyage Thither by Melville is published by Richard Bentley in London. It is a commercial disaster.
Melville's first son, Malcolm, is born.
October 11th – Melville travels to London.

1850
August 5th – Melville meets the American novelist Nathaniel Hawthorne at a picnic and they become friends.
September 14th – Melville buys Arrowhead Farm near Pittsfield, Massachusetts, using money borrowed from his father-in-law.
The Scarlet Letter, by Nathaniel Hawthorne, is published.

1851
Melville writes *Moby-Dick* and dedicates it to Nathaniel Hawthorne.
Melville's second son, Stanwix, is born.

1853
Melville's daughter, Elizabeth is born.

1855
Melville's *Israel Potter* and *Benito Cereno* are published.
Melville's daughter, Frances, is born.

1861
American Civil War begins. This inspired many of Melville's later poems.

1864
Nathaniel Hawthorne dies.
International Red Cross founded in Geneva.

1865
American Civil War ends, slavery is banned.
President Abraham Lincoln is assassinated.

1866
Melville starts work for U.S. Customs in
Manhattan.

1883
Treasure Island by Robert Louis Stevenson
published.

1885
Melville resigns as Customs Inspector.

1891
September 28th – Herman Melville dies
following heart failure. He is buried in
Woodlawn Cemetery in New York.

1924
The unfinished manuscript of *Billy Budd* is found
and published.

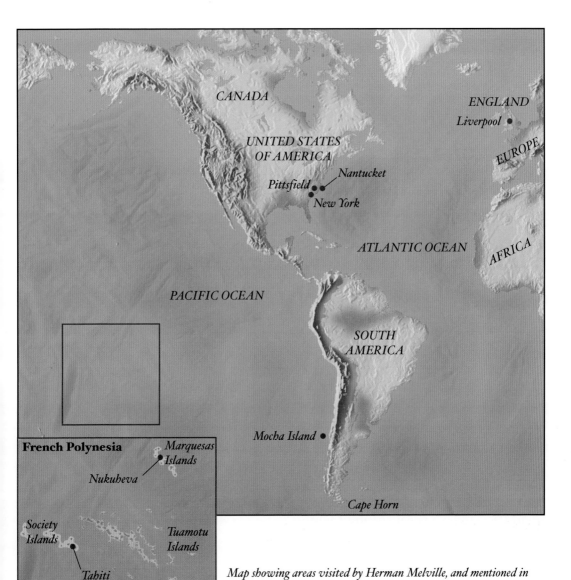

Map showing areas visited by Herman Melville, and mentioned in
Moby-Dick.

The Legacy of Moby-Dick

The Making of an American Classic

One of the greatest obstacles to Melville's success as a professional author was the lack of international copyright law at the time he was writing. This meant that American publishers could publish work by established British authors without having to pay them. Many therefore chose this option, rather than risk publishing unknown American authors whose books might not sell well, so Melville (among others) struggled to make a living as a writer. By 1847, Melville's British publisher was Richard Bentley, whose magazine first published Charles Dickens' early novels in installments. In spite of its great reputation today as an American classic, when *Moby-Dick* was first published in 1851, the first printing of 3,000 copies didn't come close to selling out.

In modern times, *Moby-Dick* has come to represent an obsessive, all-consuming pursuit which is doomed to end in failure and tragedy. To refer to someone as an "Ahab" is to accuse them of being so obsessed that they have become blind to reality, as Ahab himself was in the novel.

Literature

The French novelist Jules Verne included a search for a "Moby Dick" that sunk many ships in his novel *Twenty Thousand Leagues Under the Sea* – it turned out to be the submarine, the *Nautilus*. The novel *Ahab's Wife, or The Star-Gazer* by Sena Jeter Naslund, was inspired by Melville's brief reference to Ahab's wife (see page 33) and offers a woman's perspective of 19th-century America.

On Screen

The tale of Captain Ahab's frenzied pursuit of the white whale has inspired many artists, authors, film-makers, and musicians. The classic 1956 film adaptation starred Gregory Peck as Captain Ahab and Orson Welles as Father Mapple, and won several awards for director John Huston. There have also been radio

Gregory Peck as Captain Ahab in the 1956 film version of Moby-Dick.

plays, theatrical adaptations, Japanese cartoons, and comic books based on *Moby-Dick*.

The theme of Ahab's obsession with revenge has also appeared in both television episodes of the *Star Trek* series, and most notably in the film *Star Trek II: The Wrath of Khan* (1982).

In this, the vengeful Khan pursues the *Enterprise* and its crew through space while quoting large passages from *Moby-Dick*. A copy of the novel can even be seen on Khan's bookshelves at the start of the film. Several television movies have been made of *Moby-Dick*, the most notable being the 1998 version that starred Patrick Stewart (who also starred in *Star Trek*) as Captain Ahab.

POPULAR CULTURE

Individual characters have also become familiar in many different ways around the world, even to people who have never read the novel, through references in modern culture. For example, Agent Dana Scully on *The X-Files* named her ill-fated dog Queequeg, which is also the name of a submarine featured in the books *A Series of Unfortunate Events*. Captain Ahab himself has made appearances in films and television programs as diverse as *Futurama* and *The Pagemaster* – even appearing as a cartoon character called Moby Duck in a Disney comic book. The most well-known character from Melville's masterpiece, however, is probably Starbuck, whose name graces millions of coffee cups around the world every day.

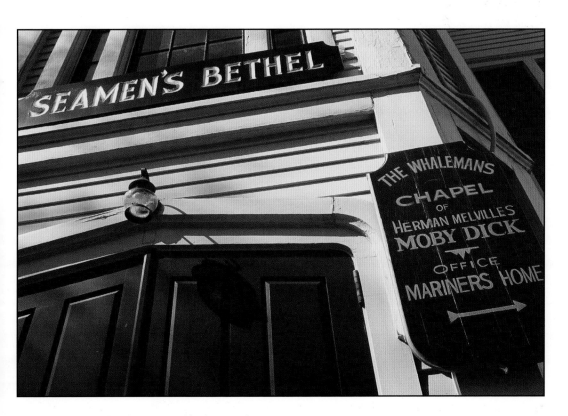

The Whaleman's Chapel in New Bedford, Massachusetts.

THE WHALING INDUSTRY

AT THE TIME OF MOBY-DICK

In Herman Melville's time, Nantucket, Massachusetts, was the center of the American whaling industry. Becoming a whaleman was considered a dangerous but glamorous profession. Payments from a whaling voyage were called "lays" and were percentages of the profit made during the voyage. By signing up for the 300th lay on the *Pequod*, Ishmael would have received 0.3% of the profits, while Queequeg the harpooner was more valuable, and would have received the 90th lay, just over 1%. The financial rewards were very low for the crews of whaling ships, who would often spend years away from home in hazardous conditions. It was not uncommon for men to desert their ships at the first port of call after discovering that a life at sea was not for them. In contrast, the owners and captains of whaling ships could make vast profits, and many of the grand houses in Nantucket and New Bedford were built with those profits.

In the 19th century, whale blubber was extremely valuable. It provided a high-quality oil that could be used in household lamps, street lamps, and even in lighthouses. In addition, it was used in factories to keep machinery running smoothly. Whalebone was used in the manufacture of umbrellas, corsets, and walking canes. However, after the discovery of petroleum in 1859, and the invention of the electric lamp in 1879, the whaling industry became outdated and whaling was phased out.

Once a whale had been killed at sea, extracting the oil from the blubber was called "trying out." The blubber was taken to the "try works" section of the ship, where it was boiled to extract the oil before being stored in barrels. The risk of fire was high on a ship covered with the highly flammable oil, so the crew had to stay alert to prevent accidents.

Spermaceti, a waxy white substance once used in cosmetics and candles, could only be obtained from sperm whales. To drain the spermaceti, a hole was cut into the whale's head and as much as 500 gallons (about 2,000 liters) could be drained from a large whale. Whales' teeth would also be pulled out and the whalemen would often carve designs or pictures of their sweethearts into them, a craft called "scrimshaw."

COURAGE AND DARING

It is a sad fact that many of the "men" sent for a life aboard Pacific whaling ships were in reality only teenage boys. The hunting methods described in *Moby-Dick* were those Melville himself would have seen

Statue of a whaler in New Bedford, Massachusetts.

on his own voyages and were extremely dangerous. A fully-grown male sperm whale can weigh up to 54 tons and measure around 55 feet (18 meters) in length, so stabbing it at close range would have required great skill and courage.

The invention of the explosive harpoon in the 1860s, which pierces the whale and then explodes, was a much more effective way of killing whales and is still used today. It is estimated that the number of sperm whales killed between 1800 and 1987 could be as high as 1,000,000.

Many countries have now signed agreements not to hunt whales because there are alternatives to the once highly-prized whale products.

Like many whale species, sperm whales were hunted so heavily that in 1970 they were declared an endangered species, and commercial hunting was banned. However, some countries, such as Japan, are granted licenses to catch limited numbers of them for scientific research.

OTHER BOOKS WRITTEN BY HERMAN MELVILLE

INDEX

FURTHER INFORMATION

IF YOU LIKED THIS BOOK, YOU MIGHT ALSO WANT TO TRY THESE TITLES IN THE BARRON'S *GRAPHIC CLASSICS* SERIES:

Treasure Island
Oliver Twist
The Hunchback of Notre Dame
Kidnapped
Journey to the Center of the Earth

FOR MORE INFORMATION ON HERMAN MELVILLE:

www.melville.org

www.mobydick.org